HUNGRY HYENA

Other books by Mwenye Hadithi and Adrienne Kennaway:

Lazy Lion
Hot Hippo
Greedy Zebra
Tricky Tortoise
Crafty Chameleon
Baby Baboon

HUNGRY HYena

By
Mwenye Hadithi

Illustrated by
Adrienne Kennaway

Hodder
Children's
Books

a division of Hachette Children's Books

One sunny day, at the lake
where Crocodile lived, Fish
Eagle caught a shiny fat fish.
Hungry Hyena lay in the papyrus.
When he saw the shiny fat fish, his
eyes grew small and greedy.

Hyena called to Fish Eagle, "Is that your nest in the big sausage tree?"
"Yes it is," Fish Eagle replied.
"Why do you ask?"

"Oh, I saw snake climbing the tree," Hyena said. "Perhaps he is looking for eagle eggs."

So Fish Eagle flew, as fast as the wind, back to her nest, leaving the shiny fat fish behind. Hyena laughed. He picked up the fish and began to eat it.

When Fish Eagle reached her nest
she saw Snake fast asleep
on a rock a long way away.

She gave a loud angry SCREECH
when she saw Hyena eating her fish. And he ate
every single bit of it.

Fish Eagle's screech woke slow, sleepy Pangolin, who was hanging by his scaly tail from the branch of a nearby bead tree. Fish Eagle told Pangolin all about Hyena's sneaky trick.

"Well, I have a
plan," said
Pangolin sleepily.
"What do hyenas
like best to eat?"

"Meat," said Fish Eagle,
"lots and lots of meat."

"Well, I think you can show them the biggest, sweetest piece of meat in all the world," said Pangolin.

And he whispered his plan to Fish Eagle.

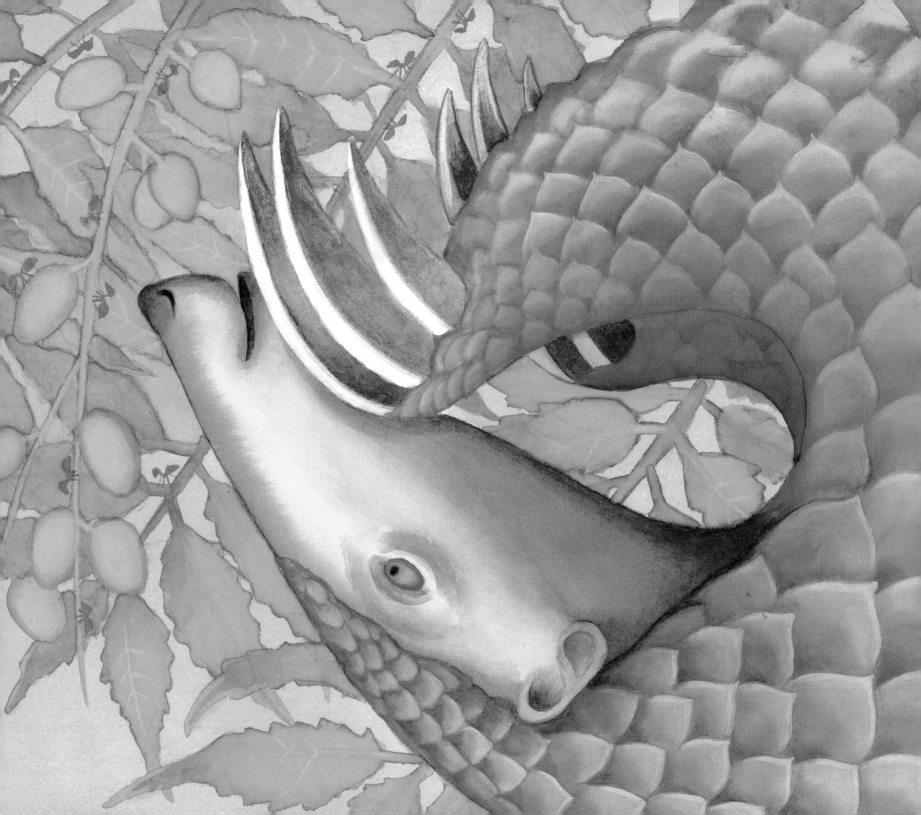

Next day Fish Eagle asked the buzzing
bees for a piece of honeycomb. Then
she flew to the water's edge where the
animals were drinking. Hyena was
pretending to be asleep.

Fish Eagle dropped the honeycomb and said loudly,
"I have found the sweetest
meat in all the world."

When Hyena heard this, he ran swiftly. For in those days he could run like the wind. "Give it to me!" cried Hungry Hyena, and he grabbed the honeycomb and swallowed it down. Every single bit of it. "Delicious! That's the sweetest meat I have ever tasted!" Hyena said, licking his lips. "I want more!"

"I know where you will find the biggest, sweetest piece
of meat in all the world," said Fish Eagle.
"There will be more than enough for you and your family
and all your friends. Bring them to the lake tonight,
every single one of them."

That night Fish Eagle waited with
Pangolin in the sausage tree. They waited
and they watched. And as the sun set,
they saw Hyena come over the hill. Behind
him was another hyena, and another,
and another, until all the hyenas had come
to the lake. Every single one of them.
"Look at the sky!" whispered Fish Eagle.

And as the full moon rose, huge and shining, Fish Eagle called, "See! There it is! Now climb on to each other's backs. You must climb up until you can reach the sweet meat in the sky!"

And the hyenas began to scramble on to each other's backs, climbing higher and higher and higher.

"Now, take the meat!" called Fish Eagle. And as the highest hyena reached out towards the moon, they all began to fall, and suddenly all the hyenas were falling out of the sky like giant raindrops.

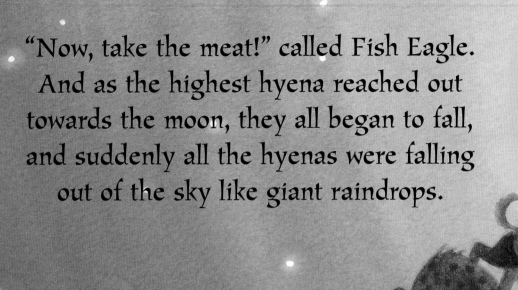

They fell heavily. And they all fell into
the lake where Crocodile lived, every single
one of them. Crocodile woke up and chased
them out of the water, biting their tails.
And when they looked up and saw the huge
white moon shining overhead, they saw
how stupid and greedy they had been,
and they all limped off into the night.

From that day on Hyena could never again run like the wind, so now he slinks about on the great African plain. And Fish Eagle soars in the clouds, and gives a screech when she remembers how the hyenas fell like raindrops from the sky,

every single one of them. . .

A catalogue record for this book is available from the British Library

ISBN 978 0 340 62685 6

Text copyright © Bruce Hobson 1994
Illustrations copyright © Adrienne Kennaway 1994

First published 1994
This edition published 2004

15 14 13 12 11 10

Hodder Children's Books
A division of Hachette Children's Books
338 Euston Road, London NW1 3BH

Printed and bound in Hong Kong